The UPS and DOWNS of Audrey May

By Missy Mareau Garcia

THE UPS AND DOWNS OF AUDREY MAY
By Missy Mareau Garcia

Artwork and Cover design by: Tracey Taylor Arvidson
Project Management/Editor: Marcy Bradford

This book is not intended as a substitute for the medical advice of physicians.

Published by Missy Mareau Garcia
15760 Ventura Blvd.
Suite 1040
Encino, CA 91436-3088
audreyandlizzie@gmail.com

ISBN 13: 9781797819662

Printed in the United States of America

For
Ava, Vivi, and Violet

Chapter One

Exactly one week before her first day of third grade, Audrey woke up to the sensation of breath on her cheek—bad breath.

"Audwey," Lizzy loudly whispered. "Are you awake? Are you? Are you? Are you?!"

Audrey tried to muster up some irritation, but couldn't stop a giggle from slipping out, as two chubby little fingers tried to pry one of her eyes open. Three-year-old sisters could be annoying, but luckily they were also cute and funny.

"OK, Lizzy, I'm up, I'm up." Audrey yawned and stretched and rolled out of her deliciously cozy bed and onto the giggling Lizzy who slept on the trundle below. Lizzy wriggled out from under her and toddled off to find their parents, her full diaper making a squishing sound as she went.

Audrey snuggled down into Lizzy's bed pulling the covers over her head. Yikes, was she really ready for this?

Audrey's dad worked on movies, and wherever he went their whole family went. They never knew where they would go next. So up until now she had homeschooled. But this year, Dad was just hired on a big space trilogy that was shooting in California, where they lived, so Audrey was finally going to get to go to a big school with other kids. She was kind of excited, but also a little scared.

"Audrey-kins..." Audrey heard her dad standing in her doorway.

Audrey burrowed down further—hiding from her Dad was another great tradition in their family. Her dad took a few steps into the room.

"No one's here, huh? I guess I'll just make the bed, but first I think I'll just lay on it for a minute." Audrey's dad flopped down on the bed.

"Oooof!" said Audrey. "Dad! You're SQUISHING ME!" She couldn't stop her laughter.

"Audrey! Oh, is that you? I thought you were gone… you'd better get up. Today is the big school shopping day with Mom."

Audrey peeked the top of her head out of the blanket. "Uh Dad, I don't know about this school thing."

"Why's that?" asked Dad, regarding her seriously. That was a great thing about Dad. He wasn't like some grown-ups who made you feel silly for wondering about things. He really listened.

"Well, I dunno, for starters, how will Mom take care of Lizzy all by herself? And what if Mrs. Vos isn't as nice as she seems. Some grown-ups are only nice when there are other grown-ups watching them. What if she's really mean…? And what if no one likes me and I never have any friends there and..."

"Whoa Audrey, slow down, you're getting a little ahead of yourself and in the wrong direction I'd say."

"What do you mean?"

"Well, if you can't help thinking about what it's going to be like, why not go the other direction with it, like, what if Mrs. Vos is even NICER than she seems, and she doesn't even teach you anything, but just hugs you and gives you candy all day long…?"

"Dad!" Audrey laughed.

"No, I'm not done, and what if you end up with so many friends that they have to call here every night so we can schedule them in for the next day, like: 'Okay Bobby, Audrey will play with you for the first five minutes of recess, but then she has a meet and greet with Kylie and Sami so please be on time, she has a very full day.'"

"Oh Dad." Audrey sat up and hugged him.

"Seriously, it may not go perfectly, but it'll be okay. It's another adventure to add to your list. Let's get going."

Audrey joined her mother and sister at the breakfast table where Lizzy was singing to her cereal. "I love my Shereaaaaal, it's so Lalishoussss..."

Mom raised her eyebrows at Audrey and passed her the cereal. "Let's get going right after breakfast, okay?"

"Okay."

"Have you thought any more about getting your ears pierced?"

"Uh... I dunno." Audrey took a deep breath. "I want to, but I'm scared it's gonna hurt."

"It's gonna hurt, hurt, huuuuuuurt," sang Lizzy.

"Lizzy! That's enough." Audrey's mom stopped the serenade. "Why don't we get our shopping out of the way and then you can see how you feel."

That night the family met down by the beach for sushi, one of their favorite meals. Audrey and Lizzy would eat so much edamame (little green soybeans) that Dad thought for sure they would turn green.

Some of Audrey's friends couldn't believe she and Lizzy ate raw fish, but the May family had just one rule about eating. You never had to eat anything you really didn't like, but you had to try everything at least once.

"You're getting pretty good with those chopsticks!" Dad said, as Audrey half stabbed, half pinched a piece of raw tuna wrapped around a piece of avocado.

"Me too, watch dis!" said Lizzy, as she picked up one of her chopsticks with one hand, picked up a piece of fish with the other hand, shoved the fish onto the chopstick and popped it into her mouth with great flourish.

"So, how did back-to-school shopping go?" asked Dad.

"Pretty good," said Audrey, "it was easy since we got my uniform a while ago. We just needed socks and tennis shoes and some new hair clips."

"Looks like those little earlobes of yours are still free of holes," said Dad.

"Yeah, well, I just… I guess I'm not ready," said Audrey. "I'm not too big on pain."

Dad laughed. "Well after all, they're your ears, and you don't ever have to pierce them if you don't want to."

"Yeah, that's the thing, I do want earrings, but you know how scared I am of needles, a needle attached to a gun?!" Audrey's face showed her horror at the thought. "I want the earrings, but not the pain."

"If only life worked like that," agreed Dad. "Now, let's finish up and go through a drive thru and get some ice cream, I hear that's still pain free!"

Audrey laughed. "Okay, but can I get french fries?' Her dad shook his head, "Yes you little weirdo.

Who doesn't like ice cream?!"

Audrey shrugged. "Dad! I like what I like and it's not sweets."

He smiled. "She likes what she likes."

Chapter Two

Audrey couldn't believe she was already finished with her first week of school. So far, she really liked it. She had made friends with Dylan, another girl who just moved to California from New York. Audrey's dad had worked on a few movies there so they had lots to talk about.

Her teacher, Miss Vos, was really nice, but pretty strict, there were some crazy boys that she had to wrangle, so you really couldn't blame her for that.

Every Friday night, the May family would lay a big blanket out on the living room floor, order takeout Thai food and watch a movie. But first Audrey had to finish cleaning up the room that she and Lizzy shared.

Audrey pushed the trundle bed that Lizzy slept on under hers and then smoothed out her own bed, looking around for Tallulah, the bear she'd had since she was a baby.

Huh, Audrey wondered, where could she be? "MOM!" she yelled, "I can't find Tallulah!"

"Oh Audrey," said Mom. "I'm sure she is right where you left her."

"Well, I slept with her last night and I haven't seen her since," Audrey said.

"Just come help me lay out the blanket. The Thai food will be here any minute. I'm sure we'll find her before you go to bed."

"Okay," said Audrey, but she had a bad feeling in the pit of her stomach.

Several hours later, the May family was very full

and very tired. The credits had just finished on the movie they watched. And they ALWAYS watched the credits. That was the only way you could see the names of all the people who had worked so hard on the movie.

Whenever they watched a show that Audrey's dad worked on, they would cheer when his name rolled past. But tonight Mr. May didn't even make it to the end of the movie... he was really tired. In fact, he was snoring on the floor, while Lizzy lay next to him imitating his loud snores and giggling. Audrey giggled too, but then she remembered. Tallulah!

"Mom, we still have to find Tallulah," she said.

Audrey's mom sighed, "Oh honey, it's so late, can we look for her tomorrow?"

Audrey's eyes filled with tears, which she tried to blink back. "Momma, I've never gone to sleep without Tallulah before."

"Okay sweetie, let's find her," her mother said.

Audrey's mother began searching the house from top to bottom. They looked behind the couch, they looked all over Audrey's room. They EVEN looked in the bathroom. Which Audrey thought was crazy since she never ever took Tallulah out of her room.

Everywhere they looked, Lizzy followed them, imitating everything they did, moving pillows they had just moved, giggling and saying, "Nope. Not there!"

After half an hour of looking, Audrey's mom hugged her hard and said, "I just don't understand it Audrey, we've looked everywhere. I'm so sorry, but I think we'll have to start again in the morning."

Lizzy let out a big yawn and said, "She sure will taste good by then!"

Mom and Audrey's heads flew around to look at Lizzy. "What did you say?!" they said in unison.

"Uh oh," said Lizzy as she clamped one of her little hands over her mouth and darted out of the room.

"Elizabeth Katherine May, you had better get your bootie back in here RIGHT now!"

Ooooh, thought Audrey, when Mom busts out Lizzy's full name, she is really in trouble. Lizzy slunk back into the room with one of the pillows from the couch covering her face.

"Lizzy?"

"Mfef?" Her face was still buried in the pillow.

"Where is Tallulah?"

"Feef fif muff fofen." Lizzy buried her face deeper.

"Elizabeth, take that pillow OFF of your face and answer me!" demanded their mother.

Lizzy slowly pulled the pillow down to reveal eyes full of tears. "She's in the OVEN!"

She slumped to the ground and put the pillow over her head as Audrey and her mother ran past her into the kitchen and opened the oven, where sure enough, there was Tallulah. Thankfully the oven was off and Tallulah was perfectly fine.

Audrey hugged her close and then looked up at her mom. "Why would Lizzy DO that?"

"I don't know, but I think we'd better go talk to her." They found Lizzy, hidden under the covers of her trundle bed.

"Lizzy, can you talk to us?" asked Mom.

Lizzy peeked just one eye out from behind her blankie and said, "Yes?"

"Lizzy, how would you feel if Audrey hid your blankie from you?"

"Sad, willy sad," said Lizzy shaking her head woefully, "but I am willy sad anyway, because Audwey is GONE all the time now!" and she burst into tears.

Audrey dropped Tallulah and ran to Lizzy, she pulled her blankie off of her face and said, "Oh

Lizzy, I miss you too when I'm at school!"

Lizzy hugged her back really hard and said, "I'm sowwy Audwey, willy willy sowwy."

"It's okay," said Audrey, "I'm sorry you've felt left out. Come on, you can sleep with me tonight." Audrey took Lizzy by the hand.

Later, as she lay in bed, it was a bit crowded but Lizzy still held tightly to her hand as she snored softly beside her. Audrey hugged Tallulah with her other arm and buried her nose into the back of the bear's fuzzy head.

Chapter Three

Audrey was sitting at her desk and looking up at the clock, lunch was pretty soon but she didn't think she could make it. She raised her hand nervously.

Mrs. Vos looked at her, "Yes, Audrey?"

"I have to go to the bathroom," said Audrey.

Miss Vos stepped a little closer to Audrey's desk and lowered her voice.

"Really, Audrey?" she looked surprised. "You just went a few minutes ago, can you please wait? Lunch is in ten minutes."

Audrey was embarrassed, but said, "No, I'm sorry, I

don't think I can hold it."

"Very well, go ahead," said Mrs. Vos.

Later, after she and Dylan finished their lunch, Shane and Jack, two of the crazy boys, came over and as usual Shane asked for Audrey's cookies. Audrey never had really been very big on sweets and it didn't take him very long to zero in on it. He then invited the girls to join in their usual game of sharks and minnows.

Audrey looked over at them, "Nah, I'm okay here, you guys go."

Audrey just didn't feel like herself, she was so thirsty and tired all the time, she didn't feel like playing or anything.

Later, after school, as Audrey got into the car to head home, she said, "Mom, do you have any water?"

"Not in the car," replied her mother. "But we'll be home in just a minute."

"Noooooo!" said Audrey. "I can't wait until then, I'm really, really thirsty, my throat feels like it's cracking. How will you feel if I die of thirst before we get home?!"

"Oh Audrey, that's quite dramatic—sheesh!" Her mom rolled her eyes. "We will be home in a minute!"

Audrey slumped into the window whimpering, "Well, please hurry, because I also have to go to the bathroom really bad."

When they got home, Audrey ran past Lizzy and into the bathroom. After she had gone to the bathroom and washed her hands, she stuck her head directly under the faucet and drank and drank and drank.

That night, while Lizzy snored on the trundle below her, Audrey just couldn't seem to fall asleep. She didn't feel good, but she didn't know how to explain it to her parents. And she was THIRSTY again, but a little nervous about getting up, because Dad had told her to stay in bed. After a few minutes, she crept into the bathroom and drank as much water as she could hold, then scurried back to her bed and finally, fell asleep.

The next morning, when Audrey woke up, she knew something was wrong. Her bed felt cold and wet. At first, she wondered if maybe Lizzy had climbed into her bed and her diaper had leaked. But when she looked down to the trundle, she could see Lizzy, sound asleep. Next, she realized that her nightgown was wet too. Had she wet the bed?! How could that be possible? She had never even had an accident before. Audrey started to cry. Just then her dad peeked his head around the corner.

"Rise and shine." But then Dad looked closer. "You okay?"

Audrey burst into tears and buried her head in her pillow. She couldn't tell him. It was too embarrassing.

Just then Lizzy woke up, looked around and said, "Peeee Yeeeww, stinky, stinky!"

Mr. May quickly figured out what was happening and sent Lizzy out of the room. "Audrey, did you have an accident?" Her dad looked surprised.

"Yes," Audrey's eyes were wide, "I don't know how it happened, I've NEVER wet the bed!"

"Listen, don't worry about it, I'm sure you're just overtired from starting school and everything. You go hop in the shower and I'll get these sheets in the wash."

By the time Audrey was dressed and ready for school, she was running late, but she sat down to eat breakfast. She took about three bites of her cereal, when it hit her. She was going to lose it. She jumped up from the table and barely made it to the bathroom in time. Vomiting is NO fun.

Her mother cleaned her up and then sent her to lay on the couch while Dad put fresh sheets on her bed. Audrey fell asleep to the sound of her parents' concerned voices in the other room.

Chapter Four

Almost a week later, Audrey was getting back into bed after vomiting AGAIN. She felt weak, shaky and THIRSTY. Always, always thirsty.

Her mom came into the room and sat on the edge of her bed. "Audrey, I just talked to Dr. Jobe, she wants us to come back in and see her today."

"Why?" asked Audrey. "I thought she said this was just a stomach virus?"

From the other room they could hear Lizzy playing her new favorite game: holding her favorite doll Emily over the toilet. "BLAAAAH, BLAAAAH, BLAAAAH!" Lizzy was getting really good at vomiting noises.

Audrey's mom gave her a weak smile, but her eyes looked worried. "This has gone on too long sweetie. Let's go see Dr. Jobe and get you better."

Audrey was scared, "I don't want to get a shot, will I have to get a shot?!"

Her mom looked at her, "I very much doubt it, now get some clothes on."

While getting dressed, Audrey pulled on her third pair of pants but just like the first two, they wouldn't stay up. This is so weird, Audrey thought to herself, these used to fit me just fine, but now, they are just too big. She finally settled on a dress and pulled on a sweater.

"I'm ready Momma."

Her mother was tying Lizzy's shoes. "Okay sweetie, let's head out to the car."

As they sat in Dr. Jobe's office Audrey just leaned on her mom, watching Lizzy play with the toys in the corner of the room. Dr. Jobe had asked her a bunch of questions and then asked her to pee in a cup, which is not an easy thing to do.

Now they were just waiting.

A few minutes later Dr. Jobe came back into the room. Something had changed, Audrey had been going to see Dr. Jobe as long as she could remember. She had never seen such a serious expression on her face. "Mrs. May, can I see you out here for a minute?"

Audrey felt nervous. Her stomach hurt, but now for a different reason. What could be wrong? She hated it when grown-ups didn't want to talk in front of her. It wasn't fair. She's the one who is sick. Was it too terrible for her to know?

Just then her mother and Dr. Jobe came back into the room. Her mother's eyes looked red, but she looked like she was trying to be brave. She sat down beside her and took one of Audrey's hands in her much larger one. "Audrey, it seems that you have something called type 1 diabetes."

Audrey felt her eyes burn as she tried not to cry. "Am I going to die, Momma??"

Audrey's mom quickly pulled her into a hug. "Oh NO, sweetie! That's not it at all, but, we do need to head to the hospital so we can get you all better. I already called Daddy and he's going to meet us here so we can all go together."

It was a long, long ride to the hospital. Dad seemed to be holding onto the steering wheel very tightly and Audrey's mother was very quiet. Audrey just looked out the window, wondering what would happen to her. She just hoped they wouldn't have to give her a shot. Shots were the scariest.

Once they arrived at the hospital everything seemed to happen very quickly. Audrey kept hearing things like "high blood glucose" and "ketones in her urine."

They put Audrey into a wheelchair and took her to a room. Her mother helped her to change into a gown and then tucked her into a hospital bed. Audrey felt SO hungry and thirsty, but no one would give her anything to eat.

Just then a kind looking nurse came into the room. "Hi Audrey, my name is Bethany and I'm your nurse. I'm going to put an IV in your arm so we can get you the medicine you need. It will hurt just a bit, so you'll have to be brave."

Audrey felt scared. She wished she could run out the room, but she felt too terrible to even fight the nurse. She started to cry and looked to her dad to rescue her.

Mr. May quickly moved to her side and took her hand. He sat down on the bed and she buried her head in his shoulder. "Let's be brave together, just hide your eyes and give the nurse your arm."

A few minutes later, the IV was in her arm, with tears drying on her cheeks, Audrey held tightly to her dad's hand and drifted off to sleep.

Chapter Five

When Audrey woke up, she was amazed to find that the IV in her arm didn't hurt at all anymore and she was starting to feel better. She looked around and saw her dad asleep in a chair on the other side of the room.

Just then, the door to her hospital room opened and her mother came in, holding a cup of coffee. She was followed by a pretty woman in a white coat carrying a clipboard.

"Audrey, you're up!" her mother was smiling. "How do you feel?"

"Better." Audrey's voice sounded cracked and dry. "Really hungry." Audrey's brow furrowed as she looked around. "Where's Lizzy?"

"She's having a sleepover with Grammy until we go home. She'll probably come visit you later today. Sweetie, this is Dr. Sibley."

"Hi Audrey." Dr. Sibley smiled at her, her long dark hair was pulled back into a ponytail and had a sparkly clip in it. "I have a few things to explain to you about how you've been feeling lately."

Audrey felt a little nervous, but she did want to know what was wrong with her. Dr. Sibley stood next to the bed and gave Audrey a paper with pictures on it.

"You see Audrey, your body needs the energy that it gets from food for you to live and play and grow. Insulin is like a magic key that unlocks the door for the good sugars in your food to go into your body. That's how your body gets energy.

Before you had diabetes, your pancreas, which is an organ in your body, like your heart or your stomach, made insulin all by itself. When a person has type 1 diabetes, their pancreas stops making insulin. That's why you've been feeling so bad. All of the sugar from the food you've been eating, has been stuck in your blood and it's making you sick. That's why you've been so thirsty and also why you wet the bed."

"The good news is," she continued, "we can give you insulin. In fact, we've been giving it to you through your IV."

Wow, that was a lot of information to take in. Audrey's head swirled. "But I'm hungry now!"

Dr. Sibley laughed. "Don't worry Audrey, food is on the way, and you and your parents will have plenty of time to learn this new way of life."

Chapter Six

Audrey and her family spent the next two days learning all about type 1 diabetes.

They had lessons with a nutritionist and learned about hidden sugars and how to count the carbohydrates in Audrey's food. They had classes with the nurses so that they could learn how to prick Audrey's finger just enough to get a drop of blood so they could measure the amount of sugar in her blood. Audrey would need to check her blood glucose about six times a day.

But probably the scariest part for Audrey, was when she and her parents had to learn how to measure the insulin into a syringe and then give her a shot. Audrey watched in horror as the nurse drew insulin up into the needle and then plunged it into the orange she was practicing on.

"Audrey," said the nurse, "I know this seems scary to you right now, but before you know it you'll be giving yourself around six shots a day."

Audrey burst into tears, she was tired of trying to be brave. Quickly, Mr. May picked her up in his arms and took her out of the room. Out in the hallway, he found a chair and sat down with her on his lap.

"Audrey, I know this all seems like too much for you, but here's what I think. We just need to take this one day at a time, one shot at a time and we'll get through it."

"But Daddy, when will I get better?" Audrey's voice was shaky and scared.

"Oh Audrey," her dad hugged her even harder. "Type 1 diabetes is something you have your whole life, so this is not going to go away, at least until someone finds a cure, but Mom and I will be with you every step of the way."

Just then Grammy and Lizzy came around the corner. Lizzy ran to Audrey hugging her and kissing her over and over and over.

Audrey couldn't help but laugh. "Oh Lizzy! I missed you too!"

Lizzy reached into a paper bag she was carrying and pulled out... TALLULAH! "I bringed her for you Audrey, and I was VERY careful with her too!"

Audrey hugged Tallulah close and then hugged Lizzy even harder, "You are the best sister ever."

"Yes I am," Lizzy agreed.

Mr. May looked at Grammy. "Would you please tell the nurses and Linda that we need a little break? Audrey and Lizzy and I are going to head down to the cafeteria."

As the three Mays got onto the elevator, Audrey said, "I wanna push the button! What floor?"

"The cafeteria is on the third floor, so push three and don't forget, your room is on the sixth floor. We don't want to get lost."

Audrey's dad smiled at the man who entered behind them. "What floor sir?"

"Four, please." The man looked kind, but sad.

As the elevator dinged, the doors opened at the fourth floor and Lizzy, saw a play area with an aquarium. She darted out and took off running.

Mr. May grabbed Audrey's hand and ran after Lizzy, by the time they caught up to her she was talking to a little girl in a wheelchair. She had beautiful blue eyes that almost looked too big for her face, and she was smiling at Lizzy.

"I willy like your hat!" Lizzy pointed to the scarf wrapped around the little girl's head.

"Thanks," the little girl reached up and touched the colorful scarf. "I'm Elaine and I wear this, because all my hair fell out and it keeps my head warm."

Lizzy smiled at her. "Well I like it, I want one too.

My sister, Audwey, is staying at the hospital too!"

Audrey smiled shyly at the little girl, who didn't look like she had the energy to get out of her wheelchair. "These fish are really cool, that one looks like Nemo."

Elaine's eyes lit up. "I know! That's what I call that one. And that is Claudia, and that crazy one is Miley, and I call that tiny one Lucy."

Lizzy's eyes were big "Are they YOURS?"

Elaine shook her head. "No, but I like to pretend they are. I have already been here for almost three months and they are good company."

Just then a nurse came up behind Elaine's wheelchair. "Time to go, Elaine." She gently began wheeling the chair away from the girls and Mr. May.

"Bye 'Laine," Lizzy waved. "Thanks for showing us your fish!"

Elaine smiled and waved back. "Bye."

Mr. May took Audrey and Lizzy by the hand. "Come on girls, back on the elevator, let's go find that cafeteria."

As Lizzy ran ahead again, hoping to push the button, Audrey squeezed her dad's hand and looked up at him. "Dad, what was wrong with Elaine, why is her hair falling out?"

"Well Audrey, I'm not sure, but I think this floor is where they take care of kids who have cancer, and sometimes the medicine they give you for cancer makes your hair fall out."

"But she'll get better, right?" Audrey looked worried.

"Honestly Audrey, I hope she does, but cancer is a very serious disease and sometimes you don't get better, but we'll pray she does, okay?"

"Okay, Dad," Audrey said.

Audrey was pretty quiet as they went to the cafeteria and picked out a few snacks. Lizzy got some french fries and a drink, but Audrey decided on a few free foods.

The nutritionist had taught her that any food with no carbohydrates in it was considered a free food, because Audrey could eat it without getting a shot. So things like cheese, or turkey or hot dogs were "free."

When Audrey got back to her hospital room, she looked around for her mother and found her sitting in the corner. Audrey could tell she'd been crying because her eyes were all red and there was a crumpled-up tissue in her hands.

"What's wrong, Momma?" Audrey walked closer to her mother, but felt a little unsure, she wasn't used to seeing her cry.

Her mother took her by the hand and pulled her closer to where she was sitting. "Oh Audreykins, honestly, I just wish there was some way I could take this from you, that I could be the one who to have diabetes instead."

Audrey hugged her and didn't say anything for a

minute, then she stepped away from her mother while still holding her hands.

"Mom, we met the nicest girl, her name is Elaine and Daddy thinks she might have cancer. I want to make a picture or something for her. She seemed so brave, it made me feel silly for feeling sorry for myself."

Mrs. May hugged her back. "That's sweet honey, but I think it's perfectly understandable to feel sad and afraid at first. Shots are scary and all of this is new for our family. But I'm glad you're ready to keep learning about diabetes and of course we can try to do something for your new friend."

Chapter Seven

Audrey had been home for two weeks while she got used to having diabetes and all that came with it, but now it was time to go back to school.

She was sitting at the breakfast table sipping a juice box. This diabetes thing was tricky. If she didn't have enough insulin, her blood sugar would go up, up, up, just like when she was first diagnosed, and then she felt terrible and barfy.

But then, sometimes she got too much insulin— even a drop can be too much—and that made her feel dizzy and shaky and not at all like herself. That's when she needed juice, or some kind of sugar that would bring her up fast, otherwise she might pass out.

There sure were lots of ups and downs to this new way of life!

"As soon as you're back in range, we need to get going." Audrey's mother moved quickly around the kitchen, wiping off counters and zipping everything into Audrey's lunch.

"I'm feeling better, you can check me again."

Her mom unzipped her blood-checking kit. Audrey cleaned her finger so her mom could use the little poker thingy, called a lancing device, to shoot a tiny needle into her finger.

"Ow!" Audrey yelped. A tiny drop of blood appeared on her finger and her mom scooped it into the little test strip that she had inserted into the glucose monitor.

Her mom smiled when the screen lit up, "Perfect! You're 102, shall we head out?"

Audrey looked at her. "I'm scared."

Her mom held on to her hand. "I know sweetie, but remember, for the first few weeks I'm going to come to the school and help you check your blood at recess and then I'll come again at lunch to give you your shot. We'll figure out the nurse later, so I'll be there!"

"But what if no one wants to play with me or be around me now?" Audrey asked.

"Audrey! Why would you say that? Of course they will still want to play with you."

Audrey didn't look up at her mother but just stared at her plate, pushing her eggs around in a circle. "They might be afraid of me, because I have a disease and they won't want to catch it from me."

"Oh Audrey, diabetes isn't contagious."

"What's contagious mean?"

"It means a kind of sickness that you can catch from

someone else, like a cold or the flu."

"Oh." Audrey nodded, but her face still looked confused. "But then why did I get it?"

"We honestly don't know why, it's not because of anything you did wrong or ate too much of. It doesn't even run in families. It's an autoimmune disease."

"What's that? It sounds scary!"

"Well, I'm still learning about all of it too, but your immune system is supposed to help protect you from getting sick. For some reason, yours got confused and started attacking itself."

Audrey looked offended. "What the heck? Why would it do that?"

Her mom laughed. "I don't know and neither do doctors or scientists but they are working hard to try to figure it out. But we do know for sure that it's not your fault and no amount of eating something different would have stopped this from happening."

Audrey looked relieved. "Okay, Momma."

CLICK CLACK CLICK CLACK Lizzy clomped into the room with a pair of fancy plastic princess shoes, she was decked out head to toe in dress up clothes, including a sparkly gown, a tiara and a feather boa. "I'm ready to take Audwey to school, Momma."

Audrey and her mother burst into laughter.

"You sure are," her mother said.

As they drove up to the school, Audrey had big butterflies in her stomach. She was pretty nervous, even though she wanted to believe her mother that everything would be okay.

When they got out of the car, she put on her backpack and then held tightly to her mother's hand, as Lizzy click clacked ahead of them in her fancy shoes.

As soon as they reached the playground, Audrey was surrounded by all of her friends.

"Audrey, we missed you!" Dylan hugged her.

"Man, oh man, you must've been really sick. You were gone FOREVER!" Shane said.

The bell rang and they all ran to line up. Audrey hugged her mom and ran to join her friends.

Later, when it was lunch time, Audrey went to the office where her mother was waiting for her. A few other kids were in the office, including Shane, who was holding an ice pack over a big bump on his forehead.

"Wow," Audrey said. "You okay?!"

"Oh this?" said Shane sheepishly. "Sharks and minnows took a bad turn today, but I'll get 'em tomorrow!"

Audrey tried not to laugh, but it was hard with Shane smirking at her.

"Come on Audrey, let's do this," her mom said. Audrey turned to where her mother was waiting with her blood check kit.

They checked her blood sugar, just like they had earlier at breakfast. Next, they looked at Audrey's lunch so Audrey could decide exactly how much she thought she could eat. Then, they had to figure out how much insulin she would need to put into the shot, so that her body would be able to use the food for energy.

Audrey felt a little funny knowing everyone might be watching her, especially Shane, but she tried not to think about it.

"Ready Audrey?" her mother had the needle all ready to go.

Audrey rolled up her sleeve and then squeezed her eyes together really tight. "Yes, go! But count one-two-three first!"

"Okay," Audrey's mom said. "One, two, three." Her mother slid the needle into Audrey's upper arm and pushed the insulin into her arm. Audrey let out a big breath and then smacked herself in the arm.

"COOL!!" It was Shane, looking right at her. "I can't believe you didn't even CRY! You have to be the bravest girl I've ever seen!"

Audrey laughed and then thought to herself, I AM brave, and smiled back him.

Chapter Eight

A few weeks later, as Audrey was getting into the car after school, her mother could tell something was wrong.

"Wanna play pwincesses when we get home?" Lizzy, buckled into her car seat, was dressed in a Dorothy costume, from The Wizard of Oz, little ruby slippers and all.

"Uh, not today Lizzy." Her mind was clearly somewhere else.

"Everything okay?" her mother asked.

"Uh, yeah… no… I don't know." Audrey let out a big sigh.

"What is it, sweetie?"

"Well, tomorrow is the Christmas party at school."

"And? That's supposed to be a good thing, right?" her mother looked confused.

"Yes, but they are going to have Christmas tree cupcakes and…" Audrey looked at her mother.

"Audrey you know you're allowed to have a cupcake, you'll just have to have an extra shot to help your body handle the extra sugar."

"I know, I just can't decide if it's really worth it, I'm already getting so many, yesterday I had SIX!"

"I understand Audrey, it's totally up to you."

"I know," sighed Audrey. "Sometimes I wish it wasn't."

Audrey was pretty quiet that night during dinner and then she went straight to bed the first time her mother asked her, which had to be a first.

The next morning when she woke up, she still wasn't sure what she wanted to do.

Later as her mother dropped her off at school, Mrs. May said, "I'll see you at lunch and then you can let me know what you want to do about the party and the cupcakes."

The morning flew by as the kids first did an art project and then cleaned up the classroom to get it ready for the Christmas break. Audrey was having fun, but in the back of her mind she couldn't stop thinking about the cupcake and the shot.

At lunchtime when she met her mom in the office and checked her blood sugar, she still felt unsure. "Okay sweetie, decision time." Her mother said, "I need to know now if you need me to come back during the party, otherwise I'll just see you after school as usual."

Audrey bounced around in a circle trying to make herself decide. She thought of the cupcake, she thought of the shot, and finally she said, "I wanna do it Momma."

"Okay, my girl,' her mother looked proud. "I'll see you in a few hours."

Later, when the party started and Mrs. Vos began passing out the Christmas tree cupcakes, her mother appeared at the door, motioning to Audrey. Mrs. Vos smiled at her and waved for her to go to her mother.

Outside the classroom, Audrey wiped her sweaty hands on her pants, she couldn't believe she was choosing to get an extra shot, but those cupcakes looked good.

"Ready, Audrey?" her mother asked.

Audrey raised her sleeve and squeezed her eyes shut. "Yes, Momma. One, two, three—GO!"

And just like that, it was over. Audrey hugged

her mother and ran into the classroom to eat her cupcake.

As she sat down next to Shane, he looked at her with wide eyes. "I thought my mom told me that people with diabetes can't eat cupcakes."

Audrey smiled at him, a lot of people thought that. "No, I can actually eat anything you can, I just have to make sure I get enough medicine so my body can use it the right way."

"Cool," Shane said.

A few weeks later the May family was back at their favorite sushi restaurant. Audrey was very hungry.

"Okay, Dad, I want some edamame, some miso soup and tonight I want just sashimi, because then I won't need so much insulin since it will be raw fish with no rice."

"Sounds good." Dad looked at Mom. "Got that?"

"Yes," her mother smiled. "That's ten grams of carbs

for a half a cup of edamame, about 7 grams for the miso soup, and, yep, you're right Audrey, sashimi is a free food so you won't need insulin for that."

Once Audrey had gotten her shot, she reached for the edamame, looked at her mother and started laughing. "He didn't notice, Momma."

"Notice what?" Mr. May started looking around the table.

"Audwey got her EAMMMPH." Audrey quickly clapped her hand over Lizzy's mouth, while Lizzy giggled and squirmed.

"No, no, no, don't tell me, let me guess." Audrey's dad looked at her critically. "A new haircut? Oh, wait… new… shirt?"

"No, Daddy." Audrey took the hand that wasn't over Lizzy's mouth and tucked her hair behind her ear, twinkling her eyes at him.

"Audrey!" her father gasped. "You pierced your ears!"

"Yes!" Audrey beamed at him.

"But, but... I thought you were too afraid. What changed your mind?" He still looked pretty shocked.

"Well, I used to be afraid of things that hurt—like needles, but then I realized, if I could get six or seven shots a day, I could definitely get my ears pierced."

"Pwetty, wight Daddy?!" Lizzy was gazing adoringly at her brave older sister.

"Yes, very pretty."

"And..." her mother raised her eyebrows at Audrey. Audrey looked confused for a moment. Her mother made the motion of shooting a basketball.

"OOOH! Yeah! And Daddy, today in P.E. Coach Eric said that he thought I was a NATURAL at basketball, and he asked if I wanted to maybe try out for the team next year!"

"Audrey! That's great. I'm so excited for you and...

I have some news of my own." Dad smiled and looked around the table.

"Ah you getting eawings too Daddy?" A gleeful Lizzy examined her father's ears.

"Ha ha, no, you crazy girl. I found out today, that while the movie takes a break this summer, we get to go work on a project in Romania!"

"Cool!" Audrey said. "We haven't been there yet, have we?"

"Womania? What's womania?" Lizzy scrunched up her eyebrows.

"It's a new adventure for the May family and no matter what that means, we're ready for it."

Mrs. May raised her glass. "To whatever is next as long as we stick together."

They all clinked their glasses together. Lizzy clinked hers a little too hard and water sloshed on the table as they all laughed.

Epilogue

As anyone who knows our family has probably guessed, this book is made up of more truth than fiction. Audrey and Lizzie are caricatures of my daughters Ava and Vivi, all of this happened before Violet was born. Ava was actually diagnosed at age 5 and she turned 18 this past January. I thought for those of you who don't know us, you would be happy to know that Ava (Audrey) has not just survived the ups and downs, but she is this amazing, funny, caring, incredibly talented person. Type 1 diabetes has not stopped her from pursuing any of her dreams. She's still not fond of needles...

I know that everyone's experience with being diagnosed with type 1 diabetes is different. This was our story. My hope in writing this was to create a resource for friends and family of newly diagnosed kids with type 1. A book where the kids can see themselves and where their friends can get a better understanding of what they are going through. I also want to clarify that this isn't the whole story, this is just the diagnoses. I hope to follow up with at least two more books in this series that give more detail and insight into what it's like living with this disease day in and day out. Thank you for reading!

Feel free to follow our family shenanigans on Instagram @missymareau. I would love to hear your story of ups and downs! Feel free to contact me by emailing audreyandlizzie@gmail.com.

Acknowledgments

My first thank you has to go to my husband Keith. I would never write anything but random FB posts if he didn't make me. It's amazing to not just be believed in, but pushed to keep going and not give up and by the way, thanks for marrying me. ;) And of course to my girls Ava, Viviana and Violet who inspire me and tell me when I'm funny and when I am so not.

I also have to thank my wonderful Project Manager/Editor Marcy Bradford. You are so talented and determined and I've loved working with you and learning from you and laughing with you. You're a gem. Which leads me to Tracey Taylor Arvidson, who Marcy found. Tracey, I feel like we won the lottery finding you. Your beautiful art has such sweetness and nuance. I feel like you really listened to what I was hoping for and then gave us work that exceeded our expectations.

I've heard so many horror stories about pediatricians who missed the signs, so I of course have to thank Dr. Christine V. Curtis, you always trusted my mom instincts, you checked for type 1 the first time we asked, we were SO lucky to have you. And of course our wonderful Pediatric Endocrinologist Dr. Kevin Kaiserman, you have always been so full of grace, encouragement and wisdom, and Mary Halvorson, I can't count the nights you've texted with me all night when Ava was sick. Love you dearly.

A big, big thank you to Laura Johnson Ricci and the Facebook group Parent of Type 1 Diabetics. You've all encouraged me with this book, shout-out to Sarah Guevara Kukral, who helped me come up with the book's title. This group is an amazing resource for any parent going through diagnosis, along with p.o.k.e.d - parents of kids experiencing diabetes and many others. There is no need to go through any of this alone.

I also have to thank the rest of my wonderful family, my mom Kit Hackett, who has prayed over every day that I wrote this, my new sister Sam, who I want way more time with and my brother Patrick Carson who has been my champion and given me so much genius advice with writing and marketing and well, life.

About the Author

Missy Mareau Garcia first decided to be a writer in the 6th grade when she thought it would be easier to write a book than a book report. The results were interesting, because when she didn't know what to do with a character she would just kill them off, resulting in a series of quite gruesome tragedies. But Miss Fish was a sympathetic teacher and encouraged her to keep trying. She then got sidetracked with dancing and performing for the next 20 years, met her husband, moved from Hawaii to California and began raising their three highly entertaining daughters while writing and working in the tv/film industry.

In 2005, her oldest daughter was diagnosed with type 1 diabetes. This was life changing for the whole family. Although resources have grown greatly since then, she still wanted to write a book about what it felt like for their family to go through this experience, in hopes that other kids and families in the same situation would not feel alone and also have a way to explain this new way of life to the people who love them.

45457874R00041

Made in the USA
Lexington, KY
16 July 2019